ASTRALMAGMA
MAIK WOLF

ASTRALMAGMA
MAIK WOLF

KERBER ART

Seiten/Pages 2 (Detail), 5
Roter Cluster 3
2012
Ölfarbe auf Leinwand/Oil on canvas
90 × 110 cm

Seite/Page 6
Astral Magma 1 Hund
2012
Ölfarbe auf Leinwand/Oil on canvas
60 × 60 cm

Seite/Page 7
Ballon 2 A Seele
2013
Ölfarbe auf Leinwand/Oil on canvas
65 × 80 cm

AstralMagma – Neue Arbeiten
Martin Stather

AstralMagma – New Works

Der Beobachter erwacht aus einem unruhigen Schlaf. Er streckt sich, steht auf und wirft einen vorsichtigen Blick aus der Tür. Diese befindet sich fünf Meter über Grund. Er wirft seinen Schutzanzug über und lässt die Strickleiter aus dem Eingang fallen. Behutsam klettert er hinab und schaut sich um. Zwei weitere Baumhäuser stehen in sicherer Entfernung, verwegene Konstruktionen aus Fundstücken, Resten von Gebäuden, improvisiert in den Himmel geschraubt. Es sind spärliche Reste, die von der Zivilisation übrig geblieben sind, ebenso wie Reste der Natur, die sich eher zögernd wieder neues Terrain erobert.

Maik Wolf malt Landschaften und Prospekte, die einen unwillkürlich schaudern lassen. Als Endzeitvisionen könnte man sie deuten, als Landschaften nach der großen, der endgültigen Zerstörung, nach dem Ende der menschlichen Gesellschaft, wie wir sie kennen. Ihn jedoch als Visionär endzeitlicher, kulturpessimistischer Betrachtung zu sehen, wäre gewiss eine unzulässige Verkürzung, eine Sichtweise, die ihm und seiner Kunst nur in Teilen gerecht wird. Nach seiner Aussage ist ihm der eher düstere Unterton vieler seiner Bilder meist gar nicht recht bewusst, da er eher formal an seine Malerei herangeht. Allerdings begründet die Atmosphäre des Düsteren, Geheimnisvollen eine ganz andere Ästhetik, die in der Abweichung vom vordergründig Schönen ihre Eigenheit entdeckt.

L'histoire, c'est moi

Die Geschichte der Landschaftsmalerei ist eine lange und wechselvolle. Ursprünglich war Landschaft nur möglich durch religiöse Bindung, Maria und Josef bei der Rast etwa, Kreuzigungsszenen, Sodom und Gomorrha. Dann werden die biblischen Szenen kleiner, marginaler, verschwinden beinahe in der Landschaft und schließlich sind sie ganz daraus verschwunden. Joachim Patinir ist einer der Ersten, die Landschaft pur für sich in den Kanon ihrer Malerei aufgenommen haben. Höfische Konfigurationen übernehmen alsbald den Platz der religiösen Szenen, aber auch Jahreszeitenbilder und Ansichten eines imaginierten irdischen Paradieses, Arkadien, bereichern das Sujet. Dann, Schluss mit dem Erhabenen, kommt der Realismus und zeigt Natur und von Menschen geformte Landschaft abseits idealistischer Prägung: Bonjour Monsieur Courbet.

Am Ende des 19. Jahrhunderts verändert sie sich wiederum – nicht-realistische, expressiv gefärbte Subjektivität übernimmt das Ruder, wird im Kubismus allansichtig

---

An observer awakens from a restless sleep. He stretches, rises and casts a wary glance through the doorway—five meters above the ground. After throwing on his protective suit, he lowers the rope ladder fastened at the entrance. Then climbing down with tentative steps, he carefully surveys the scene. Two further tree houses are visible from the still safe distance; daredevil constructions made of found materials and architectural ruins wrench their way provisorily toward the heavens. These are the sparse vestiges of civilisation, and the last remains of nature have begun, albeit hesitantly, to reclaim parts of the terrain.

Maik Wolf paints landscapes and sceneries that send shudders through the beholder. One might be wont to interpret them as end-time scenarios or landscapes from after the final, momentous destruction—the dissolution of human society as we know it. Viewing them as visionary apocalyptic, culturally pessimistic contemplations, however, would mean subscribing to an invalid abridgement—accepting a point of view that would do only little justice to Wolf and his work. Indeed, he pays, according to the artist himself, no great heed toward the rather dismal undertone inherent to many of his paintings and tends, instead, to approach his work from a set of formal considerations. Even so, the gloomy, cryptic atmospheres engender an entirely new aesthetic—one which establishes its singularity through inquisitive deviation from what is ostensibly beautiful.

L'histoire, c'est moi

The history of landscape painting is long and varied. Originally, landscape was possible only in connection with religious themes—as with Mary and Joseph's Rest on the Flight into Egypt for example, in portrayals of The Crucifixion, or depictions of Sodom and Gomorrah. The biblical scenes then become reduced, more marginal. Eventually engulfed by the landscape, they finally disappear altogether. Joachim Patinir is one of the first to have adopted the pure landscape into the canon of painting. Though the religious motifs are replaced by courtly configurations, depictions of the seasons, vedute of imagined Earthly paradises and Arcadian scenes are employed to accompany the novel subject matter. Subsequently, illustriousness likewise loses its appeal, and realism emerges to reveal nature and landscapes formed by humankind, transcendent of any idealised pretensions: Bonjour Monsieur Courbet.

At the end of the nineteenth century, on the other hand, things change again; non-representational, expressively-hued subjectivity now takes the oars, becomes, in Cubism,

und im Surrealismus zur Projektionsfläche des Unterbewussten, um nur einige Spielarten zu nennen. Man kann festhalten, dass die Landschaft in der Malerei natürlich immer eine Konstruktion des Menschen ist, die mit der Natur draußen im Grunde nicht allzu viel zu tun hat. Das Bild der Landschaft ändert sich beständig mit dem Stand der gesellschaftlichen Entwicklung, den Erkenntnissen der Naturwissenschaften, der Philosophie und natürlich mit der wechselvollen Beziehung des Menschen zur Natur.

Maik Wolfs Landschaften haben die Glätte der frühen Jahre längst verloren. Rau sind sie, die Farbigkeit wie unter einer Sonne, die nicht die unsere zu sein scheint. Wolfs Landschaften weisen zahlreiche Spuren von Verletzungen auf, durch Beton, Reklameschilder, Behausungen und Zeichen, aber auch durch andere Zerstörungen, die offenbar direkt das Ökosystem betreffen. Unwirtlich ist es auf den Bildern, man zögert, sie allein mit den Augen zu betreten. Die Atmosphäre von Verlassenheit, Zerstörung und improvisierter Wiederinbesitznahme ist verstörend. Viele der Arbeiten sind durch ein sich durch die gesamte Gestaltung ziehendes, fahles Rot charakterisiert. Undurchdringlich erscheinende Wälder tauchen hin und wieder am Horizont auf, ansonsten ist die Vegetation eher spärlich zu nennen. Einzelne Buchstaben oder Wegzeichen stehen oder liegen vollkommen ohne Beziehung wie Monumente einer vergangenen Zeit herum. Die Architekturen, die sich in früheren Bildern noch auf die Erfahrungen der Moderne und Postmoderne bezogen, die teilweise mit alpenländischer oder fernöstlicher Bauweise gesampelt waren – sie sind auf eine beinahe erschreckende Art und Weise rudimentär geworden, back to basics, manches Mal der Schwerkraft auf absurd anmutende Art und Weise trotzend. Aber auch der Mensch ist zurück in Maik Wolfs Bildern – zögerlich, klein wie eine Randbemerkung, aber er ist wieder da.

Hier und heute

Die Konzentration auf eine in den neueren Bildern durchscheinende Monochromie, die jedoch immer gebrochen wird, schafft eine Intensität des Ausdrucks, gemeinsam mit einem Farbauftrag, der brüchig und rissig daherkommt, die lang anhaltend ist.

Das Entwerfen von Landschaftsprospekten ist eine für Maler immer wieder neue Herausforderung. Romantik? Out. Realismus? Was soll's. Die wahren Landschaften sind in uns allen, in unseren Vorstellungen, unseren Sehnsüchten und Ängsten. Gerne kapseln wir uns hin und wieder ab von dem, was uns tagtäglich begegnet, suchen

the object of an all seeing gaze and, in Surrealism, the projection screen for the subconscious—to name just two variants of the newer game. Certainly, one can affirm the notion that landscape in painting is, of course, always a construction of the artist—one which, ultimately, has little to do with the real nature outside. The visual and conceptual qualities of landscape painting are perpetually subject to transformation, in correlation to the state of societal development, the insights gained by the natural sciences and philosophy and, clearly, to the changing relationships between humans and nature.

Wolf's landscapes have long since lost the glossy smoothness of the early years. They have become roughened, the palettes unfolding beneath a sun that would seem to be another entirely. Wolf's landscapes now bear numerous traces of injury—in their cement, advertisement signs, dwelling spaces and digits but also through other means of obliteration that have apparently affected the larger ecological system directly. So inhospitable is the pictorial space that one hesitates to traverse it with the gaze alone. The overall atmosphere of desolation, destruction and improvised reclamation is deeply disturbing. Many of the paintings are characterised by a creeping, fallow red that seeps through the entire composition. Though what would seem to be impenetrable forests occasionally emerge upon the horizon, the vegetation tends otherwise to be rather tenuous. Single alphabet characters or other guideposts lay scattered about and refrain from establishing any relation to one another—like lonely monuments of a bygone era. The architectural structures that, in earlier works, often referenced the experiences of both modernism and post-modernism—at times juxtaposed with Alpine or Far Eastern building styles—have now become almost shockingly rudimentary: back to the basics. Whereas the force of gravity is defied to a degree that borders even on absurdity, the human figure has also, though re-emerging in his painting tentatively and included as what would appear a marginal note, regained admittance into Wolf's pictorial worlds.

Here and now

The focus in the most recent paintings upon luminous, though at times disrupted, monochromy achieves—together with the rough, rimose texture of the paint—an intensity of expression that endures.

The conception of landscape vedute presents, time and again, a new challenge to painters. Romanticism? Out. Realism? Sure. The true landscapes are inside each of us, in our preconceptions, our longings, and our fears. We take comfort, often enough, in

andere Refugien – und nehmen uns doch immer so, wie wir sind, mit im Gepäck. Finanzkrise, Fukushima, Verlust von Privatheit, überall und jederzeit erreichbar sein – die Zahl der täglichen Bedrückungen ist Legion. Kein Wunder, dass wir in einer derart von den Verwüstungen des Alltags gezeichneten Welt Abstand nehmen wollen, ein Baumhaus bauen vielleicht, die Strickleiter nur herunterlassen, wenn die Luft rein ist.

Wolfs Malerei besitzt diese einzigartige Rauheit und Qualität, die dem Betrachter sehr nahekommt – nichts wie weg; und gleichzeitig sind wir fasziniert von den Herausforderungen, denen wir uns zu stellen gezwungen sind. Wer hat kein Auto? Wer kein Mobiltelefon? Wer ist nicht bei Facebook? Die Welt ist eine permanente Baustelle und der Mensch tut sich schwer, sich in all dem Schlamassel noch bemerkbar zu machen. Oft streng zentralperspektivisch organisiert, öfter aber auch mit dezidierten Abweichungen, ziehen uns die Bilder von Maik Wolf in den Bann. Formale Fixierungen sind wichtig in seiner Malerei, aber die fest gefügte euklidische Geometrie ist ins Wanken geraten, Unregelmäßigkeiten schleichen sich ein, die Entropie hat sich eingenistet. Wie Magma bricht sich das unbewusste Darunter durch die wohlgefügte Fassade ihren Weg, schert sich nicht um das, was ist, geht seinen eigenen Weg. Jede Zeit findet zu ihrem Ausdruck, zu dem ihr gemäßen Stil. Arbeiten wie Böcklins Toteninsel und die Malerei Dürers oder Cranachs scheinen bei Wolfs Arbeiten immer wieder einmal durch. Der Weg des Malers geht über kunsthistorische Leichen, wie jede neue Generation von Künstlern für sich entscheiden muss, was Gültigkeit besitzt und was nicht. Aus seinen Bildern spricht eine gesunde Skepsis gegenüber Entwicklungen, die global sind, aber Individuen treffen. Malend hat er seinen Weg in die Jetztzeit gefunden.

withdrawing from all that we encounter each day, in shutting ourselves in to find other places of refuge, and taking ourselves, just as we are, along upon the journey. Financial crises, Fukushima, the loss of privacy, the compulsorily constant availability—the list of oppressive everyday torments is extensive. It is no wonder that we long, in a world so plagued by everyday desolations, to retreat—to build a tree house perhaps, from which we can let down the rope ladder, once the air has cleared.

Wolf's painting commands a certain inimitable rawness, a particular quality which deeply affects the beholder; we would take to our heels and are yet simultaneously fascinated by the challenges placed before us. Who has no car? Who no mobile phone? Who is not on Facebook? The world is a permanent building site, and people have a rough go, amongst all the mayhem, of being noticed at all any more. The artist's compositions often strictly organised using single-point, central perspective but also deliberate deviations, the pictures of Maik Wolf draw us directly into their intensely captivating pictorial spaces. Formally fixated structures are important in his painting, but the firmly established Euclidean geometry has begun to falter and totter. Irregularities have crept in; entropy has taken root. Like magma, the unperceived substratum has begun to burst its way through the well-hewn surface, without any regard to what might be, or to what might stand in its path. Each era will find its own expression, each its corresponding style. Pieces such as Böcklin's Isle of the Dead, the painting of Dürer or that of Cranach certainly shimmer through Wolf's work now and again. The path of the artist, stopping at nothing, is at times forged over art historical graves. Indeed, each new generation of artists must decide for themselves what might still be valid and what is no longer. Maik Wolf's paintings speak to a healthy degree of scepticism toward developments that are global and yet deeply affect individuals. For his part, he has surely painted his own way into the present.

Seite/Page 15, Einband/Cover (Detail)
Astral Magma 7 Vexiere 2
2013
Ölfarbe auf Leinwand/Oil on canvas
200 × 260 cm

Seiten/Pages 16, 12/13 (Detail)
Astral Magma 6 ZNI 2
2013
Ölfarbe auf Leinwand/Oil on canvas
140 × 180 cm

Seite/Page 17
Astral Magma 5 First
2013
Ölfarbe auf Leinwand/Oil on canvas
140 × 180 cm

Vexiere 1 ZNI 3
2013
Ölfarbe auf Leinwand/Oil on canvas
200 × 260 cm

Astral Magma 3 AE
2013
Ölfarbe auf Leinwand/Oil on canvas
80 × 90 cm

Astral Magma 4 CL
2013
Ölfarbe auf Leinwand/Oil on canvas
100×110 cm

Abgedreht
Jürgen Schilling

Far Out Stills

Autonome Topografien und architektonische Ensembles, wie sie Maik Wolf auf seinen Gemälden beschreibt, wird man in der Realität kaum antreffen. Seine surreal anmutenden Bildentwürfe sind Bühnenprospekten vergleichbar, die darauf warten, bespielt zu werden. Eine verschleierte Spannung baut sich in ihnen zögernd und hintergründig auf, um sich schließlich umso intensiver zu manifestieren. Wolf lässt Schilderungen unterschiedlich gearteter Situationen entstehen, welche die Imaginationskraft der Betrachter gleichermaßen evozieren: unspektakuläre Vorbeifahrlandschaften, bizarre Porträts nie realisierter Bauten oder illusorische Veduten. Obwohl er darauf verzichtet, narrativen Konzeptionen eine eminente Rolle einzuräumen, tendiert der Rezipient dahin, aufgrund bestimmter Indizien abgeschlossene oder im Entstehen begriffene kuriose Märchen oder düstere Schauerdramen in diese Bildwerke hineinzudenken. Die Rätselhaftigkeit seiner sich in beunruhigender Stille präsentierenden Darstellungen fasziniert, weil sie im Detail nichts Fremdes, sondern vertraute Motivik in neuem Licht, das heißt in ungewöhnlichen Konstellationen zeigen, und weil eben – wie Sigmund Freud in einer Studie konstatierte – „das Unheimliche das Heimlich-Heimische ist, das eine Verdrängung erfahren hat und aus ihr wiedergekehrt ist, und dass alles Unheimliche diese Bedingung erfüllt"[1]. Ein Bilderfinder appelliert an unsere Emotionen und entführt uns in Gefilde, die uns – vielleicht aus wirren Träumen – vertraut erscheinen, ohne dass wir ihnen nahekommen konnten, deren Existenz wir erahnen mögen, die jedoch märchenhaft, romantisch, sentimental, ironisch, emotional, provokant oder irreal verfremdet werden und uns aufgrund formaler und chromatischer Interventionen in ihren Bann ziehen. Ratlosigkeit, Beängstigendes, Beklemmendes spricht unterschwellig aus diesen Bildern und lässt – den Fotografien der Amerikaner Gregory Crewdson oder Jeff Wall in ihrer konzentrierten Intensität und Zwielichtigkeit vergleichbar – den Gedanken an dramatisch inszenierte Cine-Stills aufkommen; sie erfassen einen spezifischen Augenblick zwischen einem nicht charakterisierten Vorher und einem ungewissen Nachher – alles bleibt in der Schwebe. Auf den ersten Blick trivial erscheinende Szenerien verkehren sich ins Doppeldeutige oder ins Fantastisch-Zeitlose suggestiver allegorischer und mythologischer Fantasy-Welten. Wäre da nicht der Verzicht auf jegliche Personnage, könnte man sich in die skurrilen Quartiere von Italo Calvinos fiktiven „unsichtbaren" Städten[2] versetzt fühlen, zumal den Gemälden Maik Wolfs unabhängig von ihrer Thematik eine eigentümliche melancholische Grundstimmung zu eigen ist.

One is hardly likely, in reality, to ever encounter the kind of autonomous topographies and architectonic ensembles depicted in the paintings of Maik Wolf. His surreal pictorial conceptions are akin to stage sceneries that yet await their performers. A veiled sense of tension gradually accrues behind the scenes within them, only to then be manifested with all the more intensity. Wolf allows situations of varying natures to emerge in his depictions, which likewise evoke the imaginative powers of the beholder: unspectacular, passing landscapes, bizarre portraits of unrealised buildings or illusionary vedute. Even though Wolf refrains from granting any eminent role to narrative conceptions, recipients find their ways into these artworks on the basis of certain intimations toward curious fairy tales or dim Gothic dramas, which appear to have either reached their conclusion or to be as yet in a state of unravelling. The mysteriousness of his depictions, presenting themselves as they do amidst a disturbing silence, fascinates in that the paintings reveal not strange but rather familiar motifs in a new light or, indeed, in unusual constellations, and does so precisely because— as established in an essay by Sigmund Freud—'the Unheimliche [uncanny] is the Heimlich-Heimische [intimately or secretly familiar or homelike], which, having once been suppressed, resurfaces; all that is uncanny fulfils this condition.'[1] An inventor of images panders to our emotions and abducts us into realms that may seem familiar— from mazy dreams perhaps—without allowing us to come too close. Though we may thus intuit their existence, they have also been magically, romantically, sentimentally, ironically, emotionally, provocatively or illusorily alienated and pull us into their spheres of influence by means of formal and chromatic interventions. Perplexity, something alarming and oppressive, speaks subliminally from these images—comparable, with regard to their concentrated intensity and shifty character, to the photographs of American artists Gregory Crewdson or Jeff Wall—and suggests the notion of dramatic film stills; they capture a specific moment between a non-characterized 'before' and an uncertain 'after'; everything hangs in suspension. Scenes that appear trivial at first glance suddenly shift into dualistic ambiguities or the fantastical timelessness of suggestive allegories and mythological fantasy-worlds. If not for the omission of any human figures, one might feel as though having been transported into some strange quarters in one of Italo Calvino's fictitious Invisible Cities,[2] especially in that Wolf's paintings host a peculiar basic melancholy mood that is independent of their subject matter.

Maik Wolf bereitet seine Bildfindungen akribisch mit digitalen Skizzen vor, wobei er aus einem reichhaltigen Fundus von selbst erstellten Fotografien, Architektur-Reproduktionen aus unterschiedlichen Quellen und kunsthistorisch relevantem Bildmaterial schöpft. Er kompiliert, zitiert, korrigiert, verwandelt und verarbeitet – von geradezu überschäumender Fantasie geleitet – die so erfahrenen visuellen Anregungen zu dicht verwachsenen, überraschenden Konstellationen. „Irgendwo ist ein gutes Kunstwerk eine Art Patchwork aus einer Menge von Einflüssen. Je mehr, desto besser, denn Kunst funktioniert nur über den Anspruch an Komplexität. Dabei finde ich es wenig relevant, ob das Material eigen oder angeeignet ist. Ich glaube nur zum Teil an Authentizität. Alles was Kunst ausmacht, entsteht durch das, was um sie herum existiert."[3] Indem Wolf sich bestimmte Formulierungen auswählt und innovativ in neue Zusammenhänge einfügt, organisiert er eine eigene Realität des physischen Raumes, wobei offenkundige Abweichungen von der Wirklichkeit geschickt überspielt und einer subjektiven Auffassung untergeordnet werden. Wesentlich ist ihm gleichzeitig seine sich kontinuierlich entwickelnde technische Auseinandersetzung mit Form und Farbe, das heißt die Ausbildung einer sich zunehmend freier entfaltenden malerischen Geste, welche insbesondere die Gestaltung der Binnenflächen bestimmt; sich während des Schaffensprozesses zufällig ergebende Mikrostrukturen wie Schlieren und Farbtropfen werden als gestalterische Elemente akzeptiert. „Mit der Malerei fängst du an, die Oberflächen zu transformieren und damit auch die Inhalte, weil es nicht eine Maschine ist, die ein Bild erzeugt, sondern sozusagen ein Organismus [...]. Die Malerei kann auf der Fläche die reine Idee überwinden und eine physische Präsenz erzeugen, so als würde sie sich selbst den Körper zu ihrem Geist schaffen."[4]

Vorgeblich untergeordnete, parallel hintereinander angelegte Flächen, deren Binnenräume sublim geometrisch gestaltet sind, führen das Auge des Betrachters in den Bildraum hinein. Häufig fügt Wolf verrätselte, fragmentarischen Fahrbahnmarkierungen ähnliche Buchstaben- und Zahlengruppen ein – wie sie auch als dreidimensional wirkende skulpturale Elemente zwischen den Gipfeln seiner Gebirgslandschaften auftauchen und chiffrierte Botschaften aussenden. Auch aus dem Nichts heranführende Wege erfüllen den Zweck, einen optischen Sog auf ein frontal gegebenes, zentrales und dominierendes Element auszuüben. Zumeist gewaltige, von einer sie geradezu überwuchernden Vegetation eingefasste Bauten erheben sich da – keine Signal-Bauten im Sinne einer „Look-at-me-architecture", sondern wunderliche Neuinterpretationen

Maik Wolf meticulously prepares his image conceptions by creating digital sketches, for which he draws from a rich collection of personally taken photographs, architectural reproductions from various sources and art historically relevant material. He compiles, quotes, corrects, transforms and processes his gathered visual inspirations into densely complex constellations, guided all the while by an exuberant imagination. 'At some point, a good work of art is akin to a kind of patchwork of countless various influences. The more the better; especially as art only really works when resulting from an aspiration toward a certain complexity. Whether the material that an artist works with is unique or appropriated is irrelevant. I believe only partially in authenticity. Everything that makes art what it is emerges through all that exists outside of it.'[3] Through his selection of certain formulations and his innovative insertion of them into new contexts, he organizes a new reality in terms of the physical space, wherein apparent divergences from the real world are adeptly embedded and subordinated to a subjective conception. Simultaneously essential is his continuously developing technical examination of form and colour, or his engendering of what has become an increasingly freer painterly gesture, especially with regard to his definition of interior planes; the micro structures that emerge by chance during the creative process, such as blotches or streaks of paint, are accepted as artistic means. 'In painting, you start by transforming surfaces and, with them, the content. It is not machines that produce pictures, but rather organisms, so to speak [...]. Painting can, upon the plane, overcome the pure idea and produce a physical presence, as though creating its own body for its mind.'[4]

Allegedly subordinate planes arranged in parallels, their inner areas sublimely, geometrically shaped, draw the viewer's gaze into the pictorial space. Wolf also often inserts obscure, fragmentary groups of letters and numbers, at times akin to road signs, at times appearing between the peaks of his mountainscapes in order to send out their encrypted messages as three-dimensional, sculptural elements. Paths emerging out of nowhere also serve to produce an optical undertow which thus undermines the frontally administered, centrally dominating elements. What, for the most part, are massive building structures soar upward, framed by veritably rampant vegetation—no signature buildings in the sense of any 'look-at-me architecture' but rather whimsical reinterpretations of classic forms. These modular components are interlaced with one another and placed into an unreal milieu with explicitly distorted proportions. Wolf thus creates utopian-like structures that are intricately stacked into horizontal and vertical,

klassischer Formen. Diese Versatzstücke werden miteinander verknüpft, in ein irreales Milieu platziert und die Größenverhältnisse explizit verschoben. So kreiert Wolf utopisch anmutende, komplex horizontal und vertikal verschachtelte, raumgreifend angelegte Baukörper. Ihm gelingen originelle Entwürfe, die an jene skulpturale Architektur erinnert, die als „Schubladenbauten" beginnend mit dem Zeitalter der Französischen Revolution gegen Ende des ausgehenden 18. Jahrhunderts schließlich die Architekturtheorie insbesondere des vergangenen Jahrhunderts nachhaltig beeinflusste. Künstler aller Gattungen hatten begriffen, was der Dadaist Raoul Hausmann in einem Manifest als den Weg aus der antihumanen „Archi-Tortur" forderte: Die Abkehr von der „Befriedigung der seßhaften Bedürfnisse des Bürgers [...]. Das Leben ist fantastisch. Die architekturelle Umgebung des Menschen, sie auch sei fantastisch."[5] Sicher hatten jene Künstler, die mit ihren Zeichnungen und Gemälden experimentelle, zukunftsorientierte, sozial fortschrittliche Modelle und Projekte vorschlugen und sich damit von der Tradition verabschiedeten, anderes im Sinn als jene Villen und Monumente, mit denen uns Maik Wolf konfrontiert. Seine virtuellen Gebilde sind gänzlich frei von Zwängen der Konstruktion und funktionalen Aufgaben. Angesichts seiner Gemälde scheint der Gedanke an prominente imaginäre Architekturen auf, wie sie Charles Robert Cockerell mit seinem Aquarell *The Professor's Dream*[6] aufzeigte, jene als fantastische Bühnenszenerie aufgebaute Akkumulation von Bauwerken aus allen Zeiten, deren Darstellungen sich zur Idealstadt summieren, an Thomas Coles *The Architect's Dream*[7] oder Hugh Ferriss' Hochhausvisionen[8], die den Wolkenkratzer als wehrhafte Burg oder Kathedrale die Zukunft simulierend inmitten eines Häusermeeres feiern.

Eine fahle, metallisch leuchtende Helle, mit Raffinement und Courage konträr gesetzte satte, grell aufleuchtende Farbigkeit und in Grau- und Braunstufen angelegte Flächen intensivieren den Eindruck atmosphärischer Frostigkeit, welche unerbittlich über Wolfs Bildern liegt. Einerseits wird so eine gewisse kühle Distanz zum Bildgeschehen aufgebaut und andererseits dessen mysteriöse Stimmung unterstrichen. Dadurch, dass er bereits gemalte Segmente abdeckt und dann ihre Konturen mit impulsiv gesetzten, chromatisch dem Hintergrund entsprechenden Strichfolgen definiert, setzt er sie von diesem ab und intensiviert in Zusammenspiel mit der Lichtführung spatiale Effekte. Auch auf größeren Farbzonen, die aus der Fernsicht plan erscheinen, bleibt die Handschrift des Malers deutlich nachvollziehbar. In einem Interview betont Wolf seine Affinität zur Malerei der Neuen Sachlichkeit und zum Magischen Realismus: „Die bizar-

spatially dominating architectural bodies. He achieves elegant conceptions reminiscent of those certain sculpturally architectural bodies referred to as 'terraced houses' that, originating in the late eighteenth century around the French Revolution, finally so substantially influenced architectural theory over the past century. Artists from across the various fields had recognized what was postulated in a manifesto by Dadaist Raoul Hausmann as being requisite for navigating the way out of anti-human 'architorture': the renunciation of 'the settled satisfaction of the Bourgeois [...]. Life is fantastic. The architectural surroundings of man—may they be fantastic as well.'[5] To be sure, those artists who, having bid farewell to tradition, were proposing experimentally, future-oriented, socially progressive models and projects with their drawings and paintings had other things in mind than the villas and monuments with which Maik Wolf confronts us. His virtual formations are entirely free of the constraints that would be posed by construction and functionality. When contemplating his paintings, the notion of prominent, imaginary architecture arises, as once presented by Charles Robert Cockerell in his watercolour *The Professor's Dream*[6]—that certain accumulation of buildings from across time, erected to produce a fantastic stage scenery, the representations of which, together, establish an ideal city. So too is Thomas Cole's *The Architect's Dream*[7] called to mind, or Hugh Ferriss's sky scraper visions,[8] which celebrate the highrise, simulated as a well-fortified castle or cathedral of the future amidst a sea of houses.

A sallow, metallically glowing, lucid brightness; a palette that, with refinement and courage is contrarily set to produce a sated and glaring colour-range; and the grey and brown shading of the planes all serve to intensify the impression of atmospheric frostiness that is so relentlessly cast over Wolf's images. A certain cool distance to the pictorial occurrences is thus established on the one hand, while the mysterious mood further emphasised on the other. By covering up the segments he has already painted and defining their contours with impulsively placed stroke effects in correlation to the chromaticity of the underlying layers, he sets them apart from the background and further intensifies the spatial effects in coaction with the distribution of light. Even in larger areas of colour, appearing flat from afar, the painter's hand remains clearly palpable. In an interview, Wolf emphasizes his affinity to the painting styles of New Objectivity and Magic Realism: 'The bizarre and yet likewise introverted landscape paintings of Franz Radziwill have impressed me [...] for a long time. When looking carefully at his work, it becomes evident that his shrill, poppy, almost expressive surrealism constitutes an

ren und zugleich introvertierten Landschaftsbilder von Franz Radziwill beeindrucken mich [...] schon seit langem. Wenn man genau hinsieht, findet sich sein schriller, poppiger, fast schon expressiver Surrealismus heute als ästhetisches Erbe in vielen Positionen der aktuellen Malerei. Mir gefallen oft die Künstler, die möglichst alltägliche, fast schon banale Bildinhalte künstlerisch so überhöht abbilden, dass sie das metaphysische Potenzial dieser Inhalte freisetzen. Damit lassen sie in gewisser Weise ihre Materie transparent erscheinen, wie in einem künstlerisch motivierten Drogenexperiment. ‚Das wahre Geheimnis der Welt liegt im Sichtbaren, nicht im Unsichtbaren', soll Oscar Wilde einmal gesagt haben. Meiner Ansicht nach stimmt das genau. In den starken Jahrzehnten seines Schaffens hat Radziwill diesen Spagat zwischen trivial und komplex unglaublich gut hingekriegt."[9] Mit dem 1983 verstorbenen norddeutschen Maler teilt Maik Wolf sein Interesse an der Kunst der niederländischen Malerei des 17. Jahrhunderts. Dieses offenbart sich in einer 2011/2012 entstandenen Folge von Gemälden, die Wolf durchgängig als Parnass betitelt und so einen Bezug zur mythischen Heimat der Musen konstruiert, die auf dem gleichnamigen Gebirgszug gemeinsam mit Apollon verehrt wurden. Insbesondere in seinem *Parnass 4* knüpft Wolf stilistisch an den von Rembrandt geschätzten und als frühen Vorläufer romantischer Landschaftskunst gewürdigten Hercules Seghers[10] an: Auf die Gipfel zweier einsamer, steil und unvermittelt aus einer flachen Ebene aufragender rundlich-bizarrer Bergkegel positioniert Wolf zwei baufällige Häuser, wobei ihm für das eine das Foto eines während einer Überschwemmung demolierten Wohngebäudes als Vorbild dient, dessen vordere Fassade abgesackt ist und den Blick ins Innere frei gibt. Da dieses nunmehr unbewohnbare Haus am Rande eines Abgrundes steht, wird suggeriert, dass ein Felsabbruch Ursache für diesen gravierenden Schaden gewesen sein könnte. Der zweite Häuserkomplex dagegen erscheint intakt. Auf den körperhaft begriffenen Felsen setzt sich die akribisch geschilderte Bewaldung fort, welche sich am Fuße der beiden Felskegel ausbreitet. Sie ergänzt eine Überwucherung durch Buschwerk und Moos, welche die gesamte Formation umkleidet. Unergründlich bleibt dem Betrachter, wie Menschen diese Häuser jemals errichten und wie sie deren Unzugänglichkeit überwinden konnten – insofern vergleichbar mit dem 2012 entstandenen *Roter Cluster 3* mit seinem Konglomerat von labyrinthischen, modernistisch-absurd verfügten Konstruktionselementen. Es handelt sich bei *Parnass 4* um ein morbides, Vergänglichkeit und Verfall assoziierendes Ensemble, bei dem sich – ähnlich wie bei den gestochenen Gebirgspanoramen von Pieter

aesthetic inheritance among many positions in contemporary art today. I am often quite gratified by the work of artists who portray the most possibly mundane, even almost banal, pictorial content with such inflatedness that the metaphysical potential of the subject matter is liberated. In this way, these artists allow the material they are working with to appear transparent to some extent, as though in a kind of artistically motivated drug experiment. Oscar Wilde is once to have said that the true mystery of the world is the visible, not the invisible. In my view, that is perfectly true. In the decades that marked Radziwill's strongest period, he managed this balancing of trivialities with complexities astoundingly well.'[9] With the Northern German painter (who passed away in 1983), Maik Wolf also shares an interest in the art of Dutch painting from the seventeenth century. That becomes apparent in a series of paintings from 2011 and 2012, each of which Wolf has titled Parnass [Mount Parnassus], *thus referencing the mountain range and mythical home of the muses who, together with Apollo, were worshiped there. Especially in his* Parnass 4, *Wolf links stylistically to Hercules Seghers,[10] who, already cherished by Rembrandt, is highly valued as an early pioneer of romantic landscape art: at the peaks of two lonely, bizarrely round, mountainous boulder-cones, abruptly jutting steeply upward from out of a flat plain, Wolf positions two ramshackle houses—for one of which, the photograph of a residential building demolished during a flood served as a model, its frontal façade thus having sagged to allow for a view of the building's interior. In that this house, now uninhabitable, stands at the very edge of an abyss, a landslide suggests itself as the possible cause for the grave damage. The second building complex, by contrast, appears to be intact. The fastidiously depicted afforestation beginning at the bases of the boulder formations makes its way up the faces of the corporeally steadfast cliffs and complements the overgrowth of bush and moss enshrouding the entire formation. Unfathomable for the beholder remains the question as to how any humans might have ever erected these houses, and as to how their inaccessibility might ever be overcome—a situation also present in* Red Cluster 3 *from 2012, with its conglomerate of labyrinthine, absurdly modernist-disposed construction elements.* Parnass 4 *is a morbid ensemble addressing the notions of perishability and decay, which rather imposes—similarly to certain engravings of mountain panoramas by Pieter Brueghel the Elder and, again, to the austere etchings and paintings of Seghers—the impression of standing before a barren scenery, the stage setting for an extinct culture once plagued by destructive catastrophes. Even*

Brueghel dem Älteren und eben Seghers' kargen Radierungen und Gemälden – der Eindruck aufdrängt, vor einer öden, von zerstörerischen Katastrophen heimgesuchten Kulisse einer erloschenen Kultur zu stehen. Selbst aus der Weite des grün-bläulichen Firmaments scheinen Himmelskörper signifikante Zeichen zu senden.

Dieser enigmatischen Komposition gingen Werke voraus, die zwar gleichfalls der *Parnass*-Serie zuzuordnen sind, aber sich insofern vom beschriebenen Bild unterscheiden, dass die dargestellten Gebirgsformationen zwischen hoch aufragenden, überdimensionierten, in irrealer toxischer Farbigkeit gestalteten zypressenartigen Gewächsen eingebettet sind. Die ausbalancierte, Tiefenraum schaffende Staffelung dieser erstarrt wirkenden Bäume funktioniert als Barriere vor dem Unbekannten. In den Fuße eines Berges eingelassene umbaute Öffnungen könnten ebenso als Zugänge zu unterirdischen Wohnräumen verstanden werden wie als geöffnete Kammern einer Nekropole und selbst vereinzelt zwischen gigantischen Pflanzen verstreute Zelte erscheinen als Fremdkörper in solch einer artifiziellen Naturlandschaft. Sie zeugen genauso von der – sporadischen oder ehemaligen? – Präsenz menschlicher Bewohner wie die für zusätzliche Verunsicherung verantwortlichen, zwischen den Bäumen gespannten Leinen mit Wäschestücken und bunten Luftballons. Das Empfinden formaler und inhaltlicher Nähe dieser Kompositionen zu Arnold Böcklins *Die Toteninsel* [11] – und in gewisser Weise zu Caspar David Friedrichs *Das Kreuz im Gebirge* [12] – drängt sich nicht zufällig auf – die über Maik Wolf Landschaften lastende Ruhe ist trügerisch und der Maler überlässt die Betrachter ihren individuellen Ahnungen.

from the depths of the green-bluish firmament, the heavenly bodies seem to send out significant signs.

This enigmatic composition was preceded by works that may equally be counted among the Parnassus *series, but which differ from the painting described here in that the portrayed rock formations are embedded between highly towering, oversized cypress-like plants that are rendered in irreal, toxic hues. The staggered arrangement of these seemingly stiff trees, well-balanced to create a great degree of depth, acts as a barrier to the unknown. Framed openings at the base of a mountain can be as well interpreted as entrance points to underground dwellings as they might be thought the exposed chambers of a necropolis; even tents, strewn singularly between giant plants, appear like foreign matter among the so artificially natural landscape. They attest to the—sporadic or former?—presence of human inhabitants to the same extent as do the still more unsettling laundry lines, strung as they are with pieces of clothing and colourful balloons. The perceived proximity of these compositions to Arnold Böcklin's* Toteninsel [11] *with regard to both form and content—and in a certain way also to Caspar David Friedrich's* Das Kreuz im Gebirge [12] *—is no coincidence. The serene stillness that weighs upon Maik Wolf's landscapes is deceitful, and the painter leaves the beholders to their individual forebodings.*

1 Sigmund Freud, Das Unheimliche, in: *Imago. Zeitschrift fur Anwendung der Psychoanalyse auf die Geisteswissenschaften*, V, 1919, S. 318.
2 Italo Calvino (1923–1985), *Die unsichtbaren Städte*, München und Wien 1984.
3 Maik Wolf in: Weltwandern – Ein E-Mail-Gespräch zwischen Christoph Tannert und Maik Wolf, geführt im Juni 2011, in: Maik Wolf, *Frontier Spirit*, Hrsg. B-05 Kunst- und Kulturzentrum Association e. V., Montabaur, Bielefeld 2011, S. 54.
4 Maik Wolf in: Maik Wolf im Gespräch mit Christian Schindler (Oktober 2006), in: Maik Wolf, *Falkenrot Preis*, Hrsg. Künstlerhaus Bethanien GmbH, Berlin 2006, S. 11.
5 Raoul Hausmann, Aufruf zur Fantasie, 1967, in: Dick Higgins und Wolf Vostell. *Pop-Architektur. Concept Art*, Düsseldorf 1969, s. p. (S. 155).
6 Charles Robert Cockerell (1788–1863), *The Professor's Dream*, 1948, Aquarell, Papier auf Leinwand, 141 × 199,5 cm, Royal Academy of Arts, London.
7 Thomas Cole (1801–1848), *The Architect's Dream*, 1840, The Toledo Museum of Art, Florence Scott Libbey Bequest, Toledo (OH).
8 Hugh Ferriss (1889–1962).
9 Vgl. Anm. 3, S. 53.
10 Hercules Seghers (1589/1590–1638/1639); vgl. Wilhelm Fraenger, *Die Radierungen des Hercules Seghers – Ein physiognomischer Versuch*, Herausgegeben und mit einem Nachwort von Hilmar Frank, 2. Aufl., Leipzig 1986.
11 Arnold Böcklin (1827–1901), *Die Toteninsel*, 1880, Kunstmuseum Basel; weitere Versionen: Metropolitan Museum, New York (1880), Alte Nationalgalerie Berlin – Staatliche Museen Preußischer Kulturbesitz (1883); Museum der bildenden Künste, Leipzig (1886).
12 Caspar David Friedrich (1774–1840), *Das Kreuz im Gebirge*, 1808, Staatliche Kunstsammlungen, Gemäldegalerie Neue Meister, Dresden.

1 Sigmund Freud, 'The Uncanny', Imago: Zeitschrift fur Anwendung der Psychoanalyse auf die Geisteswissenschaften [Imago. Journal for Practice of Psychoanalysis for the Humanities], vol. V (1919), 318.
2 Italo Calvino (1923–1985), Invisible Cities (1972).
3 Maik Wolf in an interview: 'Wandering through Worlds. An e-mail discussion between Christoph Tannert and Maik Wolf, conducted in June 2011', ed. B-05 Kunst- und Kulturzentrum e. V., Montabaur, Maik Wolf, Frontier Spirit (Bielefeld: 2011), 54.
4 Maik Wolf in an interview: 'Maik Wolf in a conversation with Christian Schindler', ed. Künstlerhaus Bethanien GmbH, Maik Wolf: Falkenrot Preis (Berlin: 2006), 11.
5 Raoul Hausmann, 'Aufruf zur Fantasie' [An Appeal for Fantasy], 1967, ed. Dick Higgins and Wolf Vostell, Pop-Architektur. Concept Art (Dusseldorf: 1969), 155.
6 Charles Robert Cockerell (1788–1863), The Professor's Dream, 1948, watercolour, paper on canvas, 141 × 199.5 cm, London, Royal Academy of Arts.
7 Thomas Cole (1801–1848), The Architect's Dream, 1840, The Toledo Museum of Art, Florence Scott Libbey Bequest, Toledo (OH).
8 Hugh Ferriss (1889–1962).
9 See note 3, 53.
10 Hercules Seghers (1589/1590–1638/1639); Cf. Wilhelm Fraenger, Die Radierungen des Hercules Seghers: Ein physiognomischer Versuch, ed. Hilmar Frank (with postface), 2nd edition, (Leipzig: 1986).
11 Arnold Böcklin (1827–1901), Die Toteninsel, 1880, Kunstmuseum Basel; further versions: Metropolitan Museum, New York (1880), Alte Nationalgalerie Berlin – Staatliche Museen Preußischer Kulturbesitz (1883), Museum der bildenden Künste, Leipzig (1886).
12 Caspar David Friedrich (1774–1840), Das Kreuz im Gebirge, 1808, Staatliche Kunstsammlungen, Gemäldegalerie Neue Meister, Dresden.

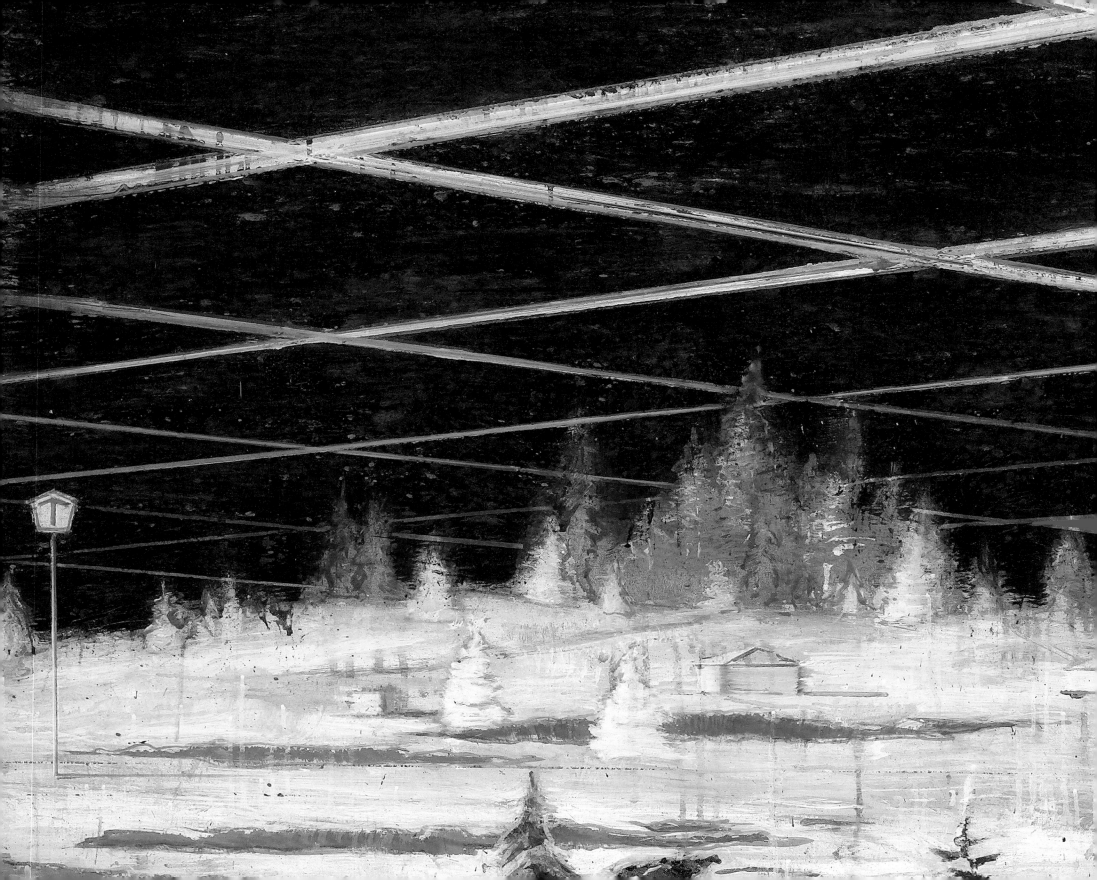

Seiten/Pages 30/31 (Detail), 19
Vexiere 1 ZNI 3
2013
Ölfarbe auf Leinwand/Oil on canvas
200 × 260 cm

Seite/Page 33
Astral Magma 2 NI
2012
Ölfarbe auf Leinwand/Oil on canvas
75 × 90 cm

Weiße Kraft 2 Monument 3
2012
Ölfarbe auf Leinwand/Oil on canvas
55×70 cm

Seite/Page 36
Munds Oxymoron 1
2012
Ölfarbe auf Leinwand/Oil on canvas
55×70 cm

Seite/Page 37
Cluster 13
2012
Ölfarbe auf Leinwand/Oil on canvas
90×110 cm

Cluster 14 Monolith 3 Nacht 2
2012
Ölfarbe auf Leinwand/Oil on canvas
200 × 280 cm

Seite/Page 40
Munds Oxymoron 2
2012
Ölfarbe auf Leinwand/Oil on canvas
65 × 80 cm

Seite/Page 41
Parnass 4
2012
Ölfarbe auf Leinwand/Oil on canvas
130 × 150 cm

Seiten/Pages 45, 42/43 (Detail)
Kryoscape 3 Frontier Spirit 2
2012
Ölfarbe auf Leinwand/Oil on canvas
150 × 200 cm

Seite/Page 46
Weiße Kraft 3
2012
Ölfarbe auf Leinwand/Oil on canvas
75 × 90 cm

Seite/Page 47
Nebel 2 RA
2012
Ölfarbe auf Leinwand/Oil on canvas
80 × 60 cm

Weiße Kraft 1
2012
Ölfarbe auf Leinwand/Oil on canvas
65 × 80 cm

333. NEF Parnass 2 Camp 1
2011
Ölfarbe auf Leinwand/Oil on canvas
200 × 270 cm

Seite/Page 52
Kryoscape 1 Parnass 3
2011
Ölfarbe auf Leinwand/Oil on canvas
90 × 110 cm

Seite/Page 53
333. NEF Parnass 1
2011
Ölfarbe auf Leinwand/Oil on canvas
260 × 200 cm

SW 1 / Haus Alles – Haus Nichts 1 / Memory Talk 1–10
2007–2009
Pigmentdruck (UltraChrome) auf Hahnemühle-Bütten
Carbon print on Hahnemühle mould-made paper
17 × 22 cm (44 × 38 cm gerahmt/framed)
Ed. 5 (2 AP)

Seiten/Pages 56/57
Sepien 1 / Die Wollust der Konzeption 1 / Chiffrierte Verse 1–20
Pigmentdruck (UltraChrome) auf Hahnemühle-Bütten
Carbon print on Hahnemühle mould-made paper
13 × 18 cm (40 × 33 cm gerahmt/framed)
Ed. 5 (2 AP)

Sapiens I / Die Wellnor der Konsumption I / Nudes & Woods I / Chilliterre Verse I

Sapiens I / Die Wellnor der Konsumption I / Reality Check II / Chilliterre Verse VIII

Sapiens I / Die Wellnor der Konsumption I / Unité – Division I / Chilliterre Verse IV

Sapiens I / Die Wellnor der Konsumption I / Nudes & Woods III / Chilliterre Verse V

Sapiens I / Die Wellnor der Konsumption I / Unité – Division V / Chilliterre Verse XX

Sapiens I / Die Wellnor der Konsumption I / Nudes & Woods VIII / Chilliterre Verse IX

Sapien I / Die Wolken der Konzeption I / Reality Check V / Chilthorne Verse XVI

Sapien I / Die Wolken der Konzeption I / Crawl – Zbrojam IV / Chilthorne Verse XV

Sapien I / Die Wolken der Konzeption I / Nuolet & Woods VII / Chilthorne Verse XI

Sapien I / Die Wolken der Konzeption I / Nuolet & Woods V / Chilthorne Verse XIV

Sapien I / Die Wolken der Konzeption I / Wälder II / Chilthorne Verse VIII

Sapien I / Die Wolken der Konzeption I / Nuolet & Woods IV / Chilthorne Verse X

Kryoscape 2 Mausoleum 5
2012
Ölfarbe auf Leinwand/Oil on canvas
100 × 130 cm

Munds Oxymoron 3
2013
Ölfarbe auf Leinwand/Oil on canvas
55 × 70 cm

ZNI 1 Ballon 1 K
2012
Ölfarbe auf Leinwand/Oil on canvas
70 × 90 cm

Weiße Kraft 4 UN
2013
Ölfarbe auf Leinwand/Oil on canvas
50×50 cm

Weiße Kraft 5 Y
2013
Ölfarbe auf Leinwand/Oil on canvas
60 × 60 cm

Seiten/Pages 66/67 (Detail)
Astral Magma 7 Vexiere 2
2013
Ölfarbe auf Leinwand/Oil on canvas
200 × 260 cm

Maik Wolf lebt und arbeitet in Berlin.
Maik Wolf lives and works in Berlin.

1964	geboren in/born in Pirna, Sachsen/Saxonia
2002 – 2007	Lehrauftrag für digitale Bildbearbeitung und Malerei/Lectureship for digital imagery and painting, EFB, Berlin
1991 – 1994	Studium an der/Studied at the École Nationale Supérieure des Beaux-Arts Paris, Frankreich/France
1987 – 1990	Studium an der/Studied at the Hochschule für Kunst und Design, Halle

Preise
Awards

2006	Falkenrot Preis/Falkenrot Prize, Berlin
2004	Arbeitsstipendium/Working grant Bemis Center for Contemporary Art, Omaha NE, USA
2003	Kunstprojekt 2003, Bega.tec, Berlin
	Kunst im Bau, GASAG, Berlin
2001	Projektförderung der/Project promotion from the Senatsverwaltung für Wissenschaft, Forschung und Kultur, Berlin
1999	1. Preis im Wettbewerb/First prize in the competition „Kunst am Bau: Neues Dresden Terminal 2001"
1995	Stipendium der/Grant from the Stiftung Kulturfonds, Berlin
	Stipendium der/Grant from the Werkstiftung Donauwörth
1994	Arbeitsstipendium der/Working grant from the Philip-Morris-Kunstförderung, Dresden
1991	Jahresstipendium des/One-year grant from the DAAD, Frankreich/France

2013	*AstralMagma*, Mannheimer Kunstverein (Kat./Cat.)
2012	*Federal Earth*, Gwangju Museum of Art, Gwangju, Korea (Kat./Cat.)
	Locked in (-) Landscapes, Jiri Svestka Gallery, Prag/Prague, Tschechische Republik/Czech Republic
	Terra Nullius, Galeria 111, Lissabon/Lisboa, Portugal
	Exterritory 2, Michael Schultz Gallery Seoul, Korea
2011	*Frontier Spirit*, b-05 Kunstzentrum Montabaur (Kat./Cat.)
	Exterritory 1, With Space Gallery, Peking/Beijing, China
	Echoland Interna, schultz contemporary, Berlin
2009	*Torpor Ultraschau*, schultz contemporary, Berlin (Kat./Cat.)
2007	*Young German Art (Vol. 1)*, Michael Schultz Gallery Seoul, Korea
	Supraficciones, Fundació „La Caixa", Lleida, Spanien/Spain (Kat./Cat.)
	Erzwungene Zukunft, Rügener Kunstverein, Puttbus
	Zehntausend Riegel, Galerie Michael Schultz, Berlin (Kat./Cat.)
2006	*Company Garden*, Brandenburgischer Kunstverein, Potsdam
	Themsetal, Galerie Alte Wache, Cuxhaven
	Falkenrot Preis, Künstlerhaus Bethanien, Berlin (Kat./Cat.)
2003	*Spätblüher*, Galerie Hartwich Rügen
2000	*Semi-Visuel*, Musée Raymond Lafage, Lisle-sur-Tarn, Frankreich/France (Kat./Cat.)
1998	*Amoureux – Bewegte Herzen II*, Galerie Hartwich Rügen (Kat./Cat.)
1997	*Amoureux – Bewegte Herzen I*, Galerie im Parkhaus, Berlin (Kat./Cat.)
1995	*In sich gerade – schräg zum Ziel*, Galerie im Parkhaus, Berlin
	Vier, Galerie Mitte, Dresden (Kat./Cat.)

2013 *Kalte Rinden – Seltene Erden*, Städtische Galerie Bietigheim-Bissingen (Kat./Cat.)
Neoexpressionism – Contemporary Art, Zhan Zhou International Cultural
and Creative Industry Park, Peking/Beijing, China (Kat./Cat.)
The Legend of the Shelves, Autocenter, Berlin
A time of gifts, Märkisches Museum Witten
Heimsuchung, Galerie Hartwich Rügen

2012 *Kalte Rinden – Seltene Erden*, Stadtgalerie Kiel (Kat./Cat.)
Kalte Rinden – Seltene Erden, Märkisches Museum Witten (Kat./Cat.)
North-East of Heaven, Galerie Hartwich Rügen
Alptraum, Goethe-Institut Johannesburg, Südafrika/South Africa
Alptraum, Green Papaya Art Projects, Quezon City, Manila

2011 *Personal Structures – Time-Space-Existence*, Collateral Event,
54. Venice Biennale (Kat./Cat.)
Alptraum, Cell Project, London
Halleluhwah! – Hommage à CAN, ABTART, Stuttgart (Kat./Cat.)
Halleluhwah! – Hommage à CAN, Künstlerhaus Bethanien, Berlin (Kat./Cat.)
HotSpot Berlin – Eine Momentaufnahme, Georg Kolbe Museum,
Berlin (Kat./Cat.)
The Solo Project, Basel, Schweiz/Switzerland (Kat./Cat.)
Alptraum, Deutscher Künstlerbund, Berlin
Discover and Escape, Orth für aktuelle Kunst / Aulich-Merkle-Stiftung,
Offenbach am Main (Kat./Cat.)
The Visitation, Galerie Hartwich Rügen
Alptraum, The Company, Los Angeles, USA

2010 *Berlin Transfer – Junge Kunst der Berlinischen Galerie und der GASAG*,
Berlinische Galerie – Museum für Moderne Kunst, Berlin (Kat./Cat.)
Constructed Landscapes, Neue Galerie Gladbeck (Kat./Cat.)
Klarland – Zweiundfünfzig Karten / Editionen, Vierter Stock Projektraum Berlin
Wachstum, Galerie Martin Mertens, München/Munich
Polyfizzyboisterous Seas, Galerie Hartwich Rügen
Alptraum, Transformer Gallery, Washington, D.C., USA

2009 *Constructed Landscapes*, Kulturspeicher Oldenburg (Kat./Cat.)
Broken Vision. Aspekte des Realismus in Malerei, Fotografie und Plastik,
Kunstverein Mannheim (Kat./Cat.)
Kunstdialog in gemeinsamer Bewegung, Wuhan Museum of Art,
China (Kat./Cat.)
Constructed Landscapes, Galerie Michael Schultz, Berlin (Kat./Cat.)
S.A.A.B.S.D.P.D.J.I.M.K.R.L.C.P.T.R.S.S.S.W.M.W., Autocenter, Berlin, und/and
Philara – Sammlung zeitgenössischer Kunst, Walzwerk, Düsseldorf (Kat./Cat.)
Foxtrott Saxonia, Kunsthalle Dresden (Kat./Cat.)

2008 *Close-Up, Por Amor à Arte Galeria*, Porto, Portugal (Kat./Cat.)

2007 *Experiment after*, Michael Schultz Gallery Seoul, Korea
Kunst im Wald, Brandenburgischer Kunstverein Potsdam
Salzmond, Kunstraum Klosterkirche, Traunstein

2006 *Sieben*, Galerie Hartwich Rügen
Planspiel_Nachspiel, Panzerhalle Potsdam

2004 *Ortsbegehung 10 / SUV*, Neuer Berliner Kunstverein, Berlin (Kat./Cat.)
Ortsbegehung 10 / SUV, Kunstverein Göttingen (Kat./Cat.)

2003 *Incidents*, Galerie & Projekte Mathias Kampl, Berlin

2002 *Große Kunstausstellung*, Haus der Kunst, München/Munich

2001 *Flora*, Neuer Sächsischer Kunstverein, Dresden

2000 *Ausgang 10*, Galerie im Parkhaus, Berlin

1999 *Sichtverhältnisse*, Künstlerhaus Bethanien, Berlin (Kat./Cat.)
Glück und Casino, Zentrum für Kunst und Medien Adlershof, Berlin
Familienaufstellung, 2YK Galerie, Berlin
Prochains, Räume für Kunst, Basel, Schweiz/Switzerland

1998 *S.S.K.*, Berlin
Sichtverhältnisse, Centro Cultural del Conde Duque, Madrid,
Spanien/Spain (Kat./Cat.)

1994 *Salon de la Jeune Peinture*, Paris, Frankreich/France

1993 *Salon d'Art Contemporain Bagneux*, Paris, Frankreich/France
Salon des Arts Plastiques Marne-la-Vallée, Paris, Frankreich/France

Bibliografie
Bibliography

AstralMagma, Hrsg./Ed. Mannheimer Kunstverein, Bielefeld 2013

Neoexpressionism – Contemporary Art, Hrsg./Ed. Zhan Zhou International Cultural
    and Creative Industry Park, Peking/Beijing 2013

Developing Landscapes / Federal Earth, Hrsg./Ed. Gwangju Museum of Art,
    Gwangju 2012

Kalte Rinden – Seltene Erden, Hrsg./Ed. Städtische Galerie Bietigheim-Bissingen,
    Stadtgalerie Kiel und Märkisches Museum Witten, Bielefeld 2012

Frontier Spirit, Hrsg./Ed. b-05 Kunst- und Kulturzentrum Association e.V., Bielefeld 2011

Personal Structures: La Biennale di Venezia 2011, Hrsg./Ed. Global Art Affairs –
    Publishing, Bonn 2011

The Solo Project 2011, Hrsg./Ed. The Solo Project, Basel 2011

HotSpot Berlin 2011, Hrsg./Ed. Georg Kolbe Museum, Berlin 2011

Rekonstruktionen – Positionen zeitgenössischer Kunst, Hrsg./Ed. Gerhard Charles
    Rump, Berlin / Kassel 2010

Gemeinsam in Bewegung – Zeitgenössische Kunst aus Deutschland und China,
    Hrsg./Ed. Kunstmuseum Wuhan, Kunstverlag der Provinz Hubai, Wuhan 2009

Broken Vision, Hrsg./Ed. Mannheimer Kunstverein, Mannheim 2009

Torpor Ultraschau, Hrsg./Ed. schultz contemporary, Berlin 2009

Constructed Landscapes, Hrsg./Ed. Galerie Michael Schultz, Berlin 2009

S.A.A.B.S.D.P.D.J.I.M.K.R.L.C.P.T.R.S.S.S.F.W.M.W., Hrsg./Ed. Philara –
    Sammlung zeitgenössischer Kunst, Köln/Cologne 2009

Close-Up, Hrsg./Ed. Manuel Cardia, Porto 2008

Kunst im Bau – Unternehmen Kunstsammlung, Hrsg./Ed. GASAG, Berlin 2007

Supraficcions, Hrsg./Ed. Fondació „La Caixa", Lleida 2007

Zehntausend Riegel, Hrsg./Ed. Galerie Michael Schultz, Berlin 2007

Falkenrot Preis 2006, Hrsg./Ed. Künstlerhaus Bethanien, Berlin 2006

Ortsbegehung 10 / SUV, Hrsg./Ed. Neuer Berliner Kunstverein 2004

Kunstbrief 08, Hrsg./Ed. Galerie im Parkhaus, Berlin 2003

Kunst im Bau 2003, Hrsg./Ed. GASAG, Berlin 2003

Semi-Visuel, Hrsg./Ed. Musée Raymond Lafage, Toulouse 2002

Sichtverhältnisse, Hrsg./Ed. Centro Cultural Conde Duque, Madrid 1999

Malerei, Hrsg./Ed. Galerie im Parkhaus, Berlin 1997

Vier, Hrsg./Ed. Phillip-Morris-Kunstförderung, München/Munich 1995

Sammlungen
Collections

Berlinische Galerie – Museum für Moderne Kunst, Berlin
Stadtgalerie Kiel
Märkisches Museum Witten
Sammlung/Collection Manuel de Brito, Lissabon/Lisbon, Portugal
Sammlung/Collection Christiane Bühling, Berlin
Sammlung/Collection Cardia, Porto, Portugal
Sammlung/Collection Cardoso, Porto, Portugal
Sammlung/Collection Danner / Daus, Berlin
Sammlung/Collection de Knecht, Amsterdam, Niederlande/Netherlands
Sammlung/Collection Gädeke, Berlin
Sammlung/Collection Hoppe, Berlin
Sammlung/Collection Jeker, Dubai, Vereinigte Arabische Emirate/
    United Arab Emirates
Sammlung/Collection Lemberg, Erftstadt
Sammlung/Collection Bettina und Jan Uwe Lieback, Berlin
Sammlung/Collection Munoz, Madrid, Spanien/Spain
Sammlung/Collection Schlegel, Berlin
Sammlung/Collection Sperling, Mainburg
Sammlung/Collection Wendt, Berlin
Sammlung/Collection Worri Bank, Seoul, Korea

Impressum
Colophon

Diese Publikation erscheint anlässlich der Ausstellung:
*This publication has been published to accompany
the exhibition:*
AstralMagma, Mannheimer Kunstverein
20. Oktober – 24. November 2013

Mannheimer Kunstverein e.V.
Augustaanlage 58
68165 Mannheim
T +49 621 402208
F +49 621 442247
info@mannheimer-kunstverein.de
www.mannheimer-kunstverein.de

Herausgeber *Editor*
Dr. Martin Stather

Konzeption Ausstellung *Exhibiton concept*
Dr. Martin Stather

Konzeption Katalog *Catalogue concept*
Maik Wolf und/and Carsten Wolff

Autoren *Authors*
Dr. Jürgen Schilling und/and Dr. Martin Stather

Fotografie *Photography*
Jürgen Gebhardt, Berlin

Übersetzungen *Translations*
Nathan Moore, Berlin

Lektorat *Editing*
Viola van Beek, Berlin
Nathan Moore, Berlin

Design
FINE GERMAN DESIGN, Frankfurt am Main

Dank *Acknowledgements*

Für die Unterstützung und die gute Zusammenarbeit zur
Realisierung der Ausstellung und dieser Publikation gilt unser
besonderer Dank:
*For their professional support and valuable collaboration in
realising this publication, we would particularly like to extend
our gratitude to:*
Viola van Beek, Jürgen Gebhardt, Christof Kerber und dem
Team des/and the team of Kerber Verlag, Nathan Moore,
Jürgen Schilling, Michael Schultz, Martin Stather und dem
Team des/and the team of Mannheimer Kunstvereins,
Carsten Wolff

Dieser Katalog erscheint mit freundlicher Unterstützung von:
This catalogue has been made possible by the kind support of:

Ritter Sport, Waldenbuch
Mannheimer Kunstverein
Galerie Michael Schultz, Berlin | Seoul | Beijing
FINE GERMAN GALLERY, Frankfurt am Main

Die Deutsche Nationalbibliothek verzeichnet diese Publikation
in der Deutschen Nationalbibliografie; detaillierte bibliografi-
sche Daten sind im Internet über http://dnb.dnb.de abrufbar./
*The Deutsche Nationalbibliothek lists this publication in the
Deutsche Nationalbibliografie; detailed bibliographic data are
available on the Internet at http://dnb.dnb.de.*

Gesamtherstellung und Vertrieb/*Printed and published by*:
Kerber Verlag, Bielefeld
Windelsbleicher Str. 166–170
33659 Bielefeld, Germany
Tel. +49 (0) 5 21/9 50 08-10
Fax +49 (0) 5 21/9 50 08-88
info@kerberverlag.com

Kerber, US Distribution
D.A.P., Distributed Art Publishers, Inc.
155 Sixth Avenue, 2nd Floor
New York, NY 10013
Tel. +1 (212) 627-1999
Fax +1 (212) 627-9484

Kerber-Publikationen werden weltweit in führenden Buch-
handlungen und Museumsshops angeboten (Vertrieb in
Europa, Asien, Nord- und Südamerika)./*Kerber publications
are available in selected bookstores and museum shops world-
wide (distributed in Europe, Asia, South and North America).*

ISBN 978-3-86678-909-8
www.kerberverlag.com

Printed in Germany